BATMAN™ RETURNS
MOVIE STORYBOOK

Adapted by Justine Korman and Ron Fontes

A GOLDEN BOOK • NEW YORK

Western Publishing Company, Inc., Racine, Wisconsin 53404

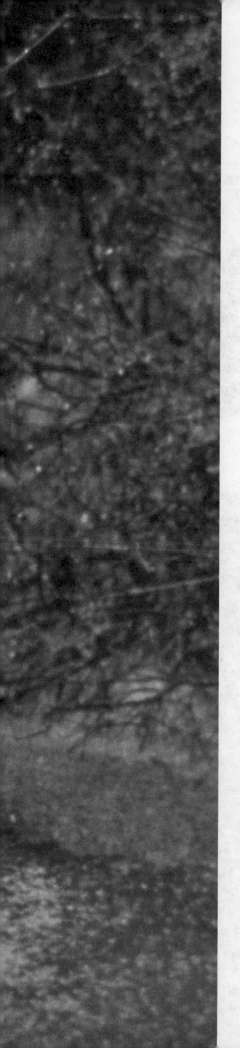

Christmas should be a time of joy. But one Christmas long ago, in Gotham City, there were two parents who were far from joyful. They had a most unusual baby boy. Instead of chubby fingers and a sweet smile, he had webbed flippers tipped with claws, a snapping beak, and an evil disposition.

Unable to live with their wicked birdbaby, the desperate parents took him to a deserted bridge in Gotham City Park. There they dumped the little creature, carriage and all, into a freezing stream.

They expected that to be the end of the nightmare—but it was only the beginning. The carriage floated through the murky waters into the ruined Gotham Park Zoo, where it came to rest on an island of ice and snow in the Arctic World Pavilion. Four majestic emperor penguins found the carriage and raised the child as their own.

Years passed, and it was Christmas again in Gotham City. In Gotham Plaza, crowds of holiday shoppers awaited the daily lighting of a giant Christmas tree. Gotham's lovely Ice Princess was ready to press the colorful button that would light the tree.

One of the shoppers in the plaza was Alfred, the butler of millionaire Bruce Wayne, who was also Batman. Alfred had noticed a bold headline in the evening paper: PENGUIN—MAN OR MYTH OR SOMETHING WORSE. Recently a rumor had been spreading about a mysterious penguinlike man living in the sewers.

"What nonsense," muttered Alfred.

Meanwhile, in his plush office above the plaza, business tycoon
Max Shreck was discussing with Gotham's mayor
Shreck's plans to build a vast power plant.

"You'll have to submit blueprints and
reports through the usual channels," the
mayor told Shreck.

Shreck's meek secretary, Selina Kyle,
said, "Um, I have a suggestion—"

"I can't listen to that now," Shreck
interrupted. As Gotham's most
prominent business leader, he was
due to make a holiday speech in
the plaza. The mayor, Shreck, and
Shreck's son, Chip, hurried off to the
tree-lighting ceremony.

Unfortunately, Shreck had left his notes behind. But before he could begin to improvise a speech, a giant Christmas present rolled into the plaza.

"Great idea," the mayor said approvingly.

"Not mine," said Shreck. He was mystified.

Suddenly the huge box burst open. Three brightly painted motorcycles roared out. Then five thugs flipped and tumbled from the box, followed by clowns, a fire breather, jugglers, an organ grinder, and even a trained poodle!

The gaudy gang leapt onto the stage and confronted the mayor's party. "We came for Shreck," said the knife thrower.

"Dad! Save yourself," shouted Chip. Max Shreck jumped from the platform and fled into the crowd.

On security duty at the scene, Police Commissioner Gordon used a radio to call headquarters. "Flash the signal!" he ordered.

In seconds the shape of a giant bat shone in the night sky, summoning Gotham's hero—Batman!

Meanwhile, Selina Kyle had rushed to Gotham Plaza with Shreck's forgotten notes. There she found a three-ring riot as the strange circus troupe terrorized the crowd of shoppers.

Just then the Batmobile roared into the plaza! With a dazzling display of clever devices, Batman began to fight the evil troupe.

A clown grabbed Selina and threatened her with a stun gun. As Batman tackled the brutal buffoon, he noticed a red triangle tattooed over the clown's left eye.

Then he noticed Selina! She and The Dark Knight locked eyes, instantly captivated by each other. With effort, Batman broke his gaze, and raced away as the crowd cheered him.

Huddled on a side street, Max Shreck also heard the cheering. Now he was safe—or so he thought. Seconds later he was pulled down a manhole!

Max Shreck awoke in a cold, dark place. He was surrounded by ice, penguins, and the troupe of odd performers—the Red Triangle Circus Gang. His bleary eyes tried to see through the gloom. There, under a grimy umbrella, was the most hideous creature Shreck had ever seen.

"You must be The Penguin!" Shreck said with a gasp. "Please don't hurt me."

"Quiet," The Penguin said as he handled a bizarre weapon shaped like an umbrella. "Odd as it may seem, we have something in common. You see, we're both monsters. But you're a well-respected monster, and I am not. Help me return to Gotham."

"I'm just a businessman," objected Shreck.

The Penguin smirked. "I know about the toxic waste from your 'clean' factory," he said. "I also have documents proving you own half the slums in Gotham City. Help me or I'll tell the public."

Shreck managed a weak smile. "Well, Mr. Penguin, *sir*, perhaps I could arrange a little 'welcome home' for you."

"You won't regret this, Mr. Shreck," The Penguin said. Then he released his wealthy prisoner.

The next night in Wayne Manor, Bruce Wayne heard some startling news on TV.

"The city will never forget this morning's miracle," the anchorman was saying. "Gotham's mystery man, The Penguin, showed himself today. He emerged from the sewers just in time to rescue the mayor's baby from a kidnapping attempt."

"All I want in return," The Penguin told the anchorman, "is to find my folks and try to understand the terrible wrong they did to a child on Christmas, long ago."

Shreck used his influence to give The Penguin access to the Gotham Hall of Records. The birdman roosted there day and night, going through the city's birth records and making a long list of names.

Meanwhile, Batman drove through Gotham's dark streets. Alfred spoke to him over the Batmobile's video telephone system. "The city has been strangely quiet since the attempted baby-napping, yet you still patrol the city," said Alfred. "What about eating and sleeping? Are you concerned about that strange, heroic penguin person?"

"Funny you should ask, Alfred," replied Batman. "Maybe I am."

Batman wasn't the only one thinking about The Penguin. All of Gotham buzzed with the birdman's sad story. Reporters and a crowd of onlookers witnessed the tragic moment when The Penguin finally found his family—in Gotham Cemetery. Playing to his audience, The Penguin forgave his parents' evil deed.

A reporter called, "Mr. Penguin!"

The little man clucked. "A penguin is a bird that cannot fly. I am a man. I have a name. My name is Oswald Cobblepot."

Deep in the Batcave, Alfred asked, "Mr. Wayne, does the phrase 'Christmas vacation' mean anything to you?"

Bruce Wayne laughed. "Listen to yourself hassling me yesterday in the car," he said. He put a disc into a CD player, and Alfred's voice came out of the speakers: ". . . What about eating and sleeping?"

Bruce Wayne clicked off the CD and returned to work. He was searching his microfiles for data on the shady Red Triangle Circus. Finally he found an old newspaper article about an aquatic "birdboy" in the circus freak show. The Red Triangle Circus had folded following reports of missing children. After that, the birdboy disappeared. Bruce Wayne realized the birdboy was none other than The Penguin.

Late that same night Selina Kyle returned home to her lonely apartment. The tired secretary took comfort from her only friend—her cat, Miss Kitty. Then Selina remembered she needed to prepare for the next day's meeting that Shreck had arranged to discuss the power plant with Bruce Wayne. Shreck wanted the millionaire to put up some of the money. Wearily, Selina went back to Shreck's office.

Several hours later Shreck found her there busily making notes from his private files. Selina innocently told him something she had discovered: The power plant would not generate power, it would *absorb* power.

Of course, Max Shreck already knew that. He was furious that Selina had discovered his secret!

"Do you know what curiosity did to the cat?" Shreck asked coldly. In a fit of rage he pushed Selina out the window.

Luckily, Selina's fall was broken by a deep snowdrift. She lay half conscious on the cold white mound, faintly calling the name of her feline friend, Miss Kitty. Soon cats of every kind and color came to Selina's rescue.

After a while she managed to pick herself up. But the woman who rose from the frozen drift was a new Selina. No longer a meek, mousy secretary, Selina Kyle had become . . . Catwoman!

At their meeting the next morning, Bruce Wayne told Max Shreck, "Gotham City has a power surplus. I'm sure you know that. So what is your angle?"

"A power surplus? What do you mean?" Shreck asked. "One can never have too much power."

"We'll find out about that," Bruce Wayne said. "Of course, I don't have a crime boss like Cobblepot in my pocket. He controls the Red Triangle Circus Gang. We both know that's true."

"I won't stand for mudslinging!" Shreck bellowed. "If my assistant were here, she'd show you the door."

To Shreck's amazement, Selina walked in. Shreck should have remembered another thing about curious cats—they have nine lives!

That night, as Catwoman prowled Gotham's back alleys, she heard a woman shrieking: "Help, Batman!" The woman had been cornered by a mugger.

Catwoman pounced on the thug. With a few expert kicks and scratches, she sent him running.

"Thank you! Thank you! I was so scared!" the woman sobbed.

But Catwoman had some angry words for the victim. "You make it so easy," she sneered. "Always waiting for some Bat*man* to save you. I am Cat*woman*. Hear me roar!"

Meanwhile at the Hall of Records, The Penguin worked on the list of names he had been compiling. Shreck came to see him there.

"How would you like to be mayor?" Shreck asked. Shreck thought if The Penguin were mayor, he'd be able to build his power plant.

"Mayor?" The Penguin's beady eyes darted greedily. Then he asked, "But aren't elections held in November?"

Shreck grinned and said, "You're right. But elected officials can be recalled. Think of it: 'Cobblepot for Mayor.' It's the destiny your parents discarded!"

"Sounds perfect!" The Penguin agreed.

Shreck explained his plan. The first step was a citywide crime wave to make the present mayor look weak. The Penguin had just the clowns for the job.

At The Penguin's command, the Red Triangle Circus Gang went on a rampage through Gotham City. They blew up bank machines and broke down shop doors. Catwoman joined the felonious fun, prowling around in the elegant Shreck's Department Store and leaving a wake of destruction.

The shopping district was in chaos by the time Batman arrived. The Dark Knight programmed his super Batarang. With a single toss, the amazing weapon knocked down the whole gang. Only the trained poodle was left standing. The dog caught the Batarang in its teeth and ran off with the weapon.

As Batman searched for his lost Batarang, he came upon The Penguin standing in front of Shreck's Department Store.

"Admiring your handiwork?" asked The Dark Knight.

The Penguin squawked indignantly. "I'm touring the riot scene, gravely assessing the devastation—upstanding mayor stuff."

"You're not the mayor," said Batman.

"Things change," The Penguin replied.

Just then Catwoman somersaulted out of the department store. Seconds later the store burst into flames with a blast that knocked both Batman and The Penguin to the ground.

The Penguin seized his chance to escape. He spun his helicopter umbrella and flew up into the air.

Meanwhile, Batman chased Catwoman up the fire escape of a nearby building. When they got to the roof, Catwoman wrapped her whip around Batman and flung him over the edge. Clinging to the whip, Batman reached into his utility belt and threw an explosive capsule at his opponent.

The blast knocked Catwoman to the ledge below. Batman leapt after her. They struggled together until Catwoman slipped over the ledge and plunged down, landing in a dump truck full of sand.

"Saved by Kitty Litter," Catwoman said with a purr. The graceful cat had now used up two lives, but she still had seven to go.

At noon the next day, The Penguin addressed a cheering crowd. He righteously accused the mayor of incompetence. After the speech The Penguin went to his grimy campaign headquarters, where Catwoman was waiting for him. She wanted to help him destroy Batman.

The Penguin cackled, "We're going to turn his spiffy Batmobile into an H-bomb on wheels. Yesterday's victor is tomorrow's vapor."

"To really destroy Batman," Catwoman said, "we must first make Gotham think he's become evil."

"You mean frame him?" The Penguin asked. "What an intriguing idea!"

Later that day Bruce Wayne met Selina Kyle in Gotham Plaza. He invited her to watch the lighting of the tree with him on the television at Wayne Manor.

Soon they were sitting together on the couch. Absorbed in conversation, they barely noticed the television until a news bulletin interrupted the show.

The anchorman announced, "The Ice Princess has been kidnapped! The police report that a blood-stained Batarang was found in her dressing room near Gotham Plaza. It looks like Batman has turned into a criminal."

Bruce hastily excused himself. Once he was out of the room, Selina rushed out, too.

Batman jumped into the Batmobile and raced to Gotham Plaza. He left the car in an alley and dashed away to find the Ice Princess.

The Red Triangle Circus Gang crept out of the shadows. This was their chance! In a wink the crafty crooks fitted the Batmobile with a remote-controlled beacon rod. They ignored the police sirens howling through Gotham Plaza.

After searching the area, Batman found the Ice Princess tied up in a deserted building.

"This was set up to look like I did it," he told the Princess as he untied the ropes around her hands. Just then Catwoman dropped down from the ceiling, where she had been hiding. She grabbed the squealing Princess and dragged her up the stairs.

Batman chased them to the roof, where The Penguin was waiting. The Penguin tossed a trick umbrella at the Princess. The umbrella opened and a swarm of baby bats flew at her.

"Don't panic!" Batman cried, and reached out to save the Princess. But it was too late! The Princess toppled from the roof.

To the horrified crowd below, it looked as if Batman had pushed the Princess to her doom! A hail of police bullets scattered across the roof and bounced off Batman's armor.

Attempting to escape the bullets, Batman fell into Catwoman's clutches. She kissed him beneath a sprig of mistletoe that hung above their heads.

Batman mused, "Mistletoe can be deadly, if you eat it."

"A kiss can be deadlier, if you mean it," Catwoman said. Then she savagely scratched at Batman's mask. Batman dove off the roof, unfurling great black gliderwings, and swooped off into the night.

The Penguin emerged and congratulated Catwoman on her victory. Then he asked her to marry him.

"I wouldn't touch you, not even to scratch you!" Catwoman snapped.

The spurned birdman sent her flying on his helicopter umbrella. Now she had used up three of her lives!

Disappointed, The Penguin returned to his campaign bus. Inside were the controls to the beacon rod hooked up to the Batmobile.

Batman's flight from the roof brought him to the Batmobile. But he was shocked to find that the powerful machine was under The Penguin's control. The speeding car roared through traffic and over sidewalks. Frantic citizens leapt from its path.

As Batman fought to control the car, The Penguin appeared on the video screen. "Welcome to the Oswald Cobblepot School of Driving," the birdman gloated.

Batman pressed a button to record The Penguin's voice.

The Penguin squawked, "Relax, and I'll take care of the wretched, pinhead puppets of Gotham."

Batman frantically tried to stop the Batmobile. He screeched to a halt in front of an old lady who stood only inches away.

Inside his bus The Penguin growled in frustration and anger. The Batmobile began moving again—speeding through the streets of Gotham completely out of control. Batman punched a hole in the floorboards, found the beacon rod, and snapped it in half. The car was once again under Batman's command.

The Penguin angrily pounded his control panel. "I came this close to a perfect evening! I iced the Princess. I almost got married. And I almost blew away Batman."

Pursued by the police and The Penguin's goons, Batman sped down an alley. Buildings at the far end of the alley formed a passage too narrow to get through! Thinking fast, Batman connected two sparking wires, causing the Batmobile's sleek sides to pop off. The Batmobile then darted easily through the space between the buildings, leaving Batman's stunned pursuers behind.

The next day The Penguin made a speech in Gotham Plaza. But the words that came out of the speakers were not what he intended. Jamming The Penguin's broadcast, Bruce Wayne played the words that he had recorded in the Batmobile during his wild ride.

"Relax, and I'll take care of the wretched, pinhead puppets of Gotham," The Penguin's recorded voice sneered.

The citizens of Gotham were outraged. A crowd of listeners chased the birdman into Gotham City Park. The Penguin dove off the same bridge his parents had thrown him over years before, and sought refuge in his chilly arctic lair.

A fat clown greeted him. "Great speech, Oswald!"

"My name's not Oswald, it's Penguin," the villain snapped. Now was the moment for his revenge. "Where's my list? Bring me the names. Gotham will never forget!"

Later that night Bruce Wayne attended Shreck's holiday Max-Squerade Ball at Shreck's Department Store. The elegant premises had been cleaned up after the fire and were filled with guests in fantastic costumes. Bruce, however, wore only an elegant tuxedo.

From across the room he saw Selina. She wasn't wearing a costume, either. Like Bruce, she was tired of wearing masks. Bruce led Selina to the dance floor. "I hoped you'd be here," he told her.

They stood beneath the mistletoe. "A kiss under the mistletoe," Selina said with a sigh. "Mistletoe can be deadly, if you eat it."

"A kiss can be deadlier, if you mean . . . it," Bruce said. They both gasped with recognition.

"You're her!" Bruce said.

"You're him!" Selina cried.

Just then an explosion ripped open the floor! The Penguin and his penguin army emerged from the hole to confront the horrified partygoers.

"Right now my troops are scouring the city, gathering Gotham's firstborn sons," the birdman announced. "I'll take this one now." He reached for Chip Shreck.

"Not Chip, please!" Max Shreck shouted. "I'm the one you want! I'm the one who set you up to be mayor."

"You have a point," The Penguin conceded. He grabbed Shreck and vanished with his victim.

"We have to do something," Selina whispered, turning to Bruce. But Bruce had slipped away in the smoky confusion.

The Red Triangle Circus Gang wound its way in a train of old circus wagons through the dark, empty streets of Gotham City. The Penguin's heartless henchmen were collecting children from their cozy beds. The Penguin's list had held the names of the firstborn sons in Gotham. His plan was to destroy them all.

"Hurry up loading those kids," the organ grinder growled.

Suddenly a shadow fell across the train's flaked paint. The organ grinder gasped as he felt himself being lifted by powerful hands. Once again, The Penguin's plans were derailed by Batman!

Shreck shivered in a cage in The Penguin's icy lair. The birdman pranced before the tycoon, twirling a musical umbrella. "A whole generation of Gotham's finest will follow me into a pool of your industrial waste," The Penguin bragged. "Then *you* will join them!"

Before The Penguin could say any more, the organ grinder's monkey hopped into the room and handed him a note:

Dear Penguin,
The children regret they are unable to attend. Have a disappointing day.
Batman

The Penguin was furious! "Thanks to Batman, the time has come to punish all of Gotham, not just its firstborn sons!" he cried.

He summoned his army of radio-controlled penguins, who were outfitted with bazooka backpacks. "Forward march!" The Penguin squawked.

As The Penguin's army waddled through the sewer pipes, the swift Batskiboat hurtled through those same dark waters. Batman whispered into his high-tech phone, "Alfred, I'm homing in on the radio signal's origin."

"Ready when you are, sir," the loyal butler replied from the depths of the Batcave.

Already the waddling horde of penguins had begun to surround Gotham Plaza. At The Penguin's electronic command, the birds would fire their bazookas.

But instead of bombing, the birds simply stood at attention. On Batman's instructions, Alfred had jammed The Penguin's signal just in time! Now in Alfred's control, the penguin army turned and marched back toward Gotham City Park.

The Penguin watched his troops on a video screen and snarled, "Who could have . . . ? Don't say it! I'm starting to lose my temper."

The Penguin grabbed an umbrella, brutally shoving aside the fat clown, who teetered and fell. Then the birdman jumped into his Duck vehicle and steered it out of the room.

The clown fell against Shreck's cage, close enough for Shreck to reach over and filch his key ring and gun. Shreck was about to escape when a cat-o'-nine-tails whip coiled around his ankles and dragged him away.

The Penguin's Duck reached the entrance to the old Arctic World Pavilion in Gotham Park Zoo just as the Batskiboat shot out of a water pipe. The two crafts collided. The Penguin jumped on Batman's back, flailing with an umbrella. Batman drew a weapon of his own—a small black device with a red light on it.

Then The Penguin saw his penguin army behind Batman. "My babies!" he squawked in confusion. Angrily, The Penguin snatched the device from Batman's grasp. He pressed the button, which opened the side panel of the Batskiboat. To his horror, hundreds of squeaky bats poured out of the Batskiboat, surrounding him. Swatting blindly, The Penguin crashed through a window and into the frozen moat.

Batman looked down at The Penguin. Then he spied Catwoman dragging Shreck toward the lair's whirring electric generator.

Just then the penguin army launched its missiles. Bombs whistled overhead, trailing smoke and fire. With a shattering boom, the old zoo burst into flames.

When the building stopped shaking, Batman swung down to join Catwoman and Shreck.

Shreck sniveled at Batman's feet. "Let's make a deal," he begged. "I'm the light of Gotham City. I can help you."

Catwoman was sure a powerful man like Shreck would never have to pay for his crimes. "The law doesn't apply to people like him!" she snarled. "Or us."

"Wrong on both counts," said Batman. Then he added tenderly, "We're the same, split down the middle. I love you, Selina."

"I love you too, Bruce," Catwoman purred. "It's just like a fairy tale. I could live with you in your castle forever. But I know I couldn't live with myself."

Shreck spoke up. "Selina? Selina *Kyle*? You're fired! Bruce *Wayne*? Why are you dressed up as Batman?"

"He *is* Batman, you moron," snapped Selina.

"He *was* Batman, you mean," said Shreck. He pulled out a gun and fired, wounding Batman. Heedless of the cat lives she was using up, Catwoman advanced on Shreck through the whizzing bullets.

"You're the light of Gotham City?" Catwoman asked the tycoon. "Then *be* the light of Gotham City." She embraced Shreck and plunged her steel talons into the electric generator. A spray of sparks and electricity blinded Batman. When the smoked cleared, Shreck was dead. And Selina had vanished!

Catwoman was gone, but The Penguin remained. Weakened by the heat, he stumbled through a rain of fiery rubble to the smoking generator.

"I must turn up the air conditioner," The Penguin moaned. "It's so stuffy in here." But he couldn't get the generator to start up again.

Then the dazed birdman noticed Batman. He fired a trick umbrella, but the parasol just spun harmlessly round and round.

"I picked the wrong one!" the birdman groaned, seeing his deadly umbrella-gun in Batman's hands. "You wouldn't blow away an endangered bird, would you?" The Penguin panted. He could hardly breathe now. He waddled toward the melting moat. "I'll murder you momentarily. But first a cool drink . . ."

The Penguin reached for the last chunk of ice. But his flippers fell short of their goal, and he collapsed in a heap inches from the ice block.

His body was solemnly borne away by the four emperor penguins that had raised him.

The next day carefree carolers once again sang in grand old Gotham. Alfred steered Bruce Wayne's Rolls-Royce down a dark alley. Bruce Wayne brooded in the backseat, but hope stirred in his heart. Perhaps Selina was still alive.

"I didn't find her, Alfred," he said. "Maybe . . ."

"Yes, maybe," Alfred agreed. "Come what may, Merry Christmas."

"Right," Bruce Wayne said glumly. "Peace on earth, goodwill toward men . . ."

Just then a loud *meow* echoed from a nearby building. A shape darted off into the shadows. Was it just a cat—or was it the woman he loved?

". . . And goodwill toward women," whispered Bruce Wayne.